D1276623

THE TECHNOLOGY OF
MESOPOTAMIA

Graham Faiella

rosen
central™

The Rosen Publishing Group, Inc., New York

For Lynn

Published in 2006 by The Rosen Publishing Group, Inc.
29 East 21st Street, New York, NY 10010

Copyright © 2006 by The Rosen Publishing Group, Inc.

First Edition

All rights reserved. No part of this book may be reproduced in any form without permission in writing from the publisher, except by a reviewer.

Library of Congress Cataloging-in-Publication Data

Faiella, Graham.
The technology of Mesopotamia/Graham Faiella.—1st ed.
   p. cm.—(The technology of the ancient world)
Includes bibliographical references and index.
ISBN 1-4042-0560-8 (library binding)
1. Technology—Iraq—History—To 634—Juvenile literature. 2. Iraq—Civilization—To 634—Juvenile literature. I. Title. II. Series.
T16.F35 2005
609.35—dc22
                                                                        2005013900

Manufactured in the United States of America

On the cover: Top: Mesopotamian artisans from around 2000 to 1595 BC crafted this baked clay model of a chariot. Bottom: This illustration of the palaces of Nimrud in Nineveh along the Tigris River appeared in *Discoveries in the Ruins of Nineveh and Babylon* (1853), which was written by Sir Austen Layard, a British archaeologist who excavated Nineveh.

CONTENTS

INTRODUCTION

MESOPOTAMIA: THE CRADLE OF CIVILIZATION

People first began settling the area we know today as Iraq, northern Syria, and southwestern Iran between 8,000 and 9,000 years ago. Their farming communities grew bigger and more complex. They built towns and cities. They developed technologies and made important inventions that we still use today. (The word "technology" comes from the Greek words *techne*, meaning "art" or "craft," and *logos*, meaning "word" or "study." It has come to mean the use of science and engineering to perform practical tasks.)

This was the land of Mesopotamia. The word "Mesopotamia" means "the land between the rivers" (the Tigris and the Euphrates). It was the first place in the world where large, complex societies used communal technology to organize themselves efficiently. Mesopotamia was the cradle of civilization.

The Mesopotamian civilization was the first to build cities. The Mesopotamians' inventions and technologies evolved with their urban life. They learned how to manufacture things; keep written records; count things and measure time; govern people; construct buildings, from ordinary houses to royal palaces; produce food efficiently in large amounts; irrigate their desert fields; and transport things—and people—across long distances.

This reconstruction of the Ishtar Gate was built in Baghdad, Iraq, to become the entrance to a museum that was never completed. The original Ishtar Gate (Ishtar was the goddess of war and love) was the eighth gate to the inner city of Babylon and was constructed around 575 BC by King Nebuchadrezzar II (circa 630–562). The original gate was built using blue glazed clay bricks and bricks that included reliefs of dragons, lions, and bulls.

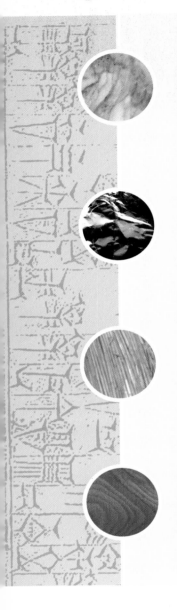

DATES FOR EVENTS IN MESOPOTAMIAN HISTORY

It is very difficult to determine accurate dates for the oldest events and periods of time in Mesopotamia. Dates have to be derived from archaeological evidence. In some cases it can only be said that an event or development happened within a thousand-year period, which is called a millennium. In those cases, it is common to date the development or event in a particular millennium BC. However, no one can say accurately, for example, when Mesopotamian cities were first built. We know only that they appeared in the fourth millennium BC (4000–3001 BC), meaning between 5,000 and 6,000 years ago. The first writing also appeared sometime in the fourth millennium, although probably closer to 3000 BC than 4000 BC.

1000 BC–1 BC	First millennium
2000–1001 BC	Second millennium
3000–2001 BC	Third millennium
4000–3001 BC	Fourth millennium
5000–4001 BC	Fifth millennium

Mesopotamia was a region dominated at different periods by various groups of people for more than 4,500 years. Each new period had its own civilization, its own capital cities, languages, gods, and dynasties of kings.

Sumer, in the south, was the first great civilization of Mesopotamia, beginning around 3500 BC. The Sumerians were followed by the Akkadians (2334–2193 BC). From about 1900 BC until 539 BC, Assyria in the north and

A map shows Mesopotamia, part of the region of what today we call the Middle East that was situated between the Tigris and Euphrates rivers, around 1750 BC when King Hammurabi ruled Babylon. The Mesopotamians were the first ancient people to keep written records and to construct cities.

MESOPOTAMIA AT THE TIME OF HAMMURABI

Later names are in parentheses

0   50   100 miles

the city of Babylon in the south were the main centers of Mesopotamian civilization.

For almost 1,000 years, between 539 BC and AD 651, foreigners from Greece and Persia ruled Mesopotamia. The invasion of Muslim Arabs in "the land between the rivers" in the AD 650s marked the beginning of Islamic civilization and the end of Mesopotamian civilization. The desert sands buried Mesopotamia's great cities. Its most important technologies, however, have survived and are in continuous use to the present day.

THE TECHNOLOGY OF MATERIALS

The most common raw materials around Mesopotamia were clay, sand, and water reeds. Copper was imported. Some of these, such as clay and copper, could be used on their own to make things with very basic technology. Tin was imported and added to copper to make bronze. The Mesopotamians could make better quality materials, such as bronze and glass, only after they had mastered the skill of controlling heat at high temperatures in ovens called kilns.

Clay

The earliest Mesopotamian technology was used for making clay pottery. It dates back more than 8,000 years. At first, Mesopotamian pottery was shaped by hand from a lump of wet clay. A potter shaped the clay into the form of whatever object the potter wanted to make. It was then left out in the desert sun to dry.

The Mesopotamians shaped clay objects and baked them hard in kiln ovens. At left, this baked clay pot had a picture of a boat engraved on it and was made around 1850 BC in the Sumerian city of Umma. At right, this glazed jar was made in the eighth century BC in the northern Mesopotamian city of Ashur and illustrates the advances in technology that had occurred by then. Potters were using many colors and glazing the pottery to ensure that liquid contents such as ointments, oils, or perfumes would not lose their aromas.

After the clay baked hard in the sun, the potter might paint a basic geometric design, human figures, or an abstract pattern of dots and strokes on it.

Sun-baked pottery absorbed liquids into the clay, causing it to crumble. Pottery for holding liquids had to be baked in a kiln at a high temperature, above 900° Fahrenheit (482° Celsius). The fierce heat of the kiln changed the chemical composition of the clay so that it did not absorb liquids.

Around 1500 BC, the Mesopotamians started making glazed pottery in kilns. They made the glaze by applying a natural substance, such as ground quartz, to the surface of the clay object. In the

This head of an Akkadian ruler, thought to be King Sargon (2334–2279 BC), was cast in bronze in Nineveh around 2200 BC. The eyes of the bronze sculpture were once inlaid with precious stones. By smelting copper and tin together, Mesopotamians made bronze, which they used for ax heads, spear heads, helmets, swords, and statues, among other items.

Metals

Copper was known in Mesopotamia from early times. The addition of tin to copper, by smelting the two metals together at a high heat, made bronze. By around 3000 BC, Mesopotamians were using bronze wherever a strong and hard metal was needed. They made bronze sockets to attach ax heads and spear heads more firmly to their wooden shafts. They made helmets, swords, body armor, statues, utensils, and tools out of bronze. Gold was used to make necklaces and other jewelry, daggers, statues of gods and goddesses, and helmets. Gold jewelry was often decorated with precious stones, such as lapis lazuli.

Glass

The Mesopotamians began making glass beads toward the end of the third millennium BC. They began making glass bottles around 1500 BC. The basic method was to melt together silica (crushed quartz and sand) with salt, ash from burnt plants, and lime. The hot liquid cooled into solid glass. To make a hollow object out of glass, they first made a mold out of mud and straw in

kiln, the quartz melted to form a hard glaze on the surface of the object. The glaze gave a higher quality finish to the object. A design glazed onto a kiln-fired object would also be more permanent. Glazed pottery also sealed in the aromas of the contents, such as scented oils and perfumes.

THE POTTER'S WHEEL

By around 3500 BC, the Mesopotamians were using a round turntable—the potter's wheel—to hold a lump of clay. They shaped the clay by hand as they turned the wheel. The potter's wheel made it possible to turn out more finely shaped pottery than the crude objects molded by hand alone.

the shape of the object. They could then dip the mold in the liquid glass, which covered the mold. When the liquid glass cooled, they could break the mold, now inside the glass object, by scraping it into small pieces with a stick and shaking the bits out.

Around 700 BC, they began using the "lost wax" technique. For this method they made an inner mold of solid clay, which they covered with wax. They covered the wax with an outer layer of clay. Small pegs connected the inner and outer molds. The pegs kept the molds together when the wax was melted away by heating up the molds. Liquid glass was poured into the space where the wax had been. When the glass cooled, the outer clay layer and inner mold were removed, leaving the hollow glass object.

The Mesopotamians blended metallic ores, such as copper or iron, with the liquid glass to make different colored glassware. Their favorite color was blue, to imitate lapis lazuli, the most popular gemstone. They only started making transparent glass around 700 BC. Glassblowing came even later, during the first century BC.

CREATING CITIES
AND BUILDINGS

People had been settling around the Euphrates and Tigris rivers since 10,000–9000 BC. The rivers were a good source of water in that desert region. Around 7000 BC, the people started farming. Agriculture led to more permanent communities. As they grew more food, the population increased. Small villages expanded in size once irrigation made agriculture more efficient.

Sometime around 5500 BC, the Mesopotamians started building bigger villages. Their villages grew into towns, which grew into cities. The earliest known Mesopotamian city was Uruk, from about 3200 BC. Eridu, which was located about 125 miles (200 kilometers) north of the mouth of the Euphrates, in southern Mesopotamia, grew from a village into a city around 3000 BC. Today the site is known as Abu Shahrein, Iraq. And so architecture was born in Mesopotamia, to build the great temples, palaces,

A wall relief from Sargon II's palace at Dur Sharrukin (Khorsabad) depicts builders constructing a village. Sargon II, who reigned from 721 to 705 BC, had his palace built northeast of Nineveh around 717–707 BC. The palace complex measured one square mile (2.59 square km). Its outer walls included seven reinforced gates.

The Nergal Gate, pictured here, has been restored in the outer wall of the city of Nineveh. Partly constructed of mud, brick, and stone, the city wall contained fifteen gates, all of which were named after Assyrian gods. Nineveh reached its peak during the reign of Sennacherib, who ruled from 704 to 681 BC.

houses, and public buildings within the world's first cities.

Clay Brick Technology

The technology used to build Eridu was basically the same for all Mesopotamian buildings: sun-dried bricks (also called mud bricks) and bundles of reeds. There was plenty of clay around to make bricks. Reeds grew in the marsh region of southern Mesopotamia. They were bundled together to reinforce the brickwork. Until the late twentieth century, the Marsh Arabs of southern Iraq still used reed bundles to build their houses.

Sun-dried bricks were used to build basic structures in Mesopotamia. Better quality kiln-dried bricks were used for more important buildings, such as temples, or for canals and dikes. Bricks dried in kilns were more durable. They were also more expensive. The Mesopotamians had to use wood to

MESOPOTAMIAN CONCRETE

At one time, around 3400 BC, at the city of Uruk, Mesopotamian builders invented a kind of concrete. This was a wet mix of gypsum and crushed baked bricks that dried hard. They used it to build the exterior of buildings. Limestone and concrete were used to make the walls in the interior. This technology was later abandoned, however, when dried mud bricks were used for all buildings.

fuel the kilns. And in most of Mesopotamia, wood was scarce.

Mud bricks were easy to make, cheap, and they provided good insulation. The main disadvantage was that they had to be protected from moisture. Otherwise they fell apart. In some places, Mesopotamian builders applied a kind of gypsum plaster on brick walls, which protected them for a while. Even with a plaster coating, however, maintenance of Mesopotamian brickwork was a constant task.

Southern Mesopotamian bricks were plano-convex, or flat on one side and rounded on the other. They were laid in a herring-bone pattern with the sides of the bricks pointing inward and outward. Plano-convex,

sun-dried mud bricks are still used in this area today.

Bitumen

Another material the Mesopotamians used in construction was bitumen, or tar, a thick, heavy crude oil that seeped to the surface of the ground as bitumen (which it still does today in the region, similar to the Rancho La Brea tar pits of downtown Los Angeles, California). The Mesopotamians spread bitumen between the foundation of a building and the bricks used for its construction. The bitumen was a waterproof seal to protect the brickwork. It was used in other kinds of construction, too, as an all-purpose waterproofing material.

The ruins of the Palace of Shapur I in Ctesiphon, Iraq, include a barrel vault and a series of arches known as blind arcades. Shapur I (AD 241–272), of the Sassanid dynasty, built this palace after he and his troops won a battle against the Romans in 244 in Ctesiphon. The Sumerians invented the arch around 3000 BC.

The Arch

The horizontal beams above doorways and passageways in Mesopotamian buildings were originally straight pieces of wood or stone. The problem was that they could only be as wide as the piece of wood or stone used. Also, all the weight of the building on top was centered on the beam of wood or block of stone. Too much weight would make it collapse. Sometime in the fourth millennium BC, the Sumerians invented the arch. It was much stronger than the simple horizontal beams they had used before. A series of arches, or vaults, could be built to make tunnels. Eventually the Mesopotamians used the same technique to build bridges and aqueducts.

Ziggurats

The Mesopotamians were famous for building ziggurats. These structures

Dwelling Places for the Gods

The largest ziggurat found so far was in Babylon. Some people believe it to be the Tower of Babel. Originally called *Etemenanki* ("the foundation of heaven and earth") in Sumerian, the ziggurat stood 300 feet (91 meters) high. The base of the ziggurat was about 660 feet (201 m) long and wide. On top of the base were seven more platforms, each smaller than the previous, like a series of huge steps. A chamber at the top was intended for use by the greatest Mesopotamian god, Marduk, as a place to sleep. Parts of the ziggurat might also have been used by Mesopotamian astronomers to observe the stars and planets, according to an account by the Greek historian Diodorus Siculus of the first century BC. Today only the foundations of the ziggurat still exist, because it was destroyed by Alexander the Great. The best preserved Mesopotamian ziggurat today is Ur, which dates from the late third millennium BC.

The ruins of the ziggurat at Ur (built around 2100 bc) are pictured here. The ziggurat, which was rebuilt several times, was around 240 feet (73 m) high. It was constructed to honor the patron god of Ur, Nanna, god of the moon.

were built in a series of rectangular tiers, or platforms. Each platform was smaller than the one below it. Most archaeologists assume that at the top of the ziggurat there was probably a shrine to a god, although no shrine has ever been found on the thirty or so ziggurats that have been discovered so far. Ramps similar to staircases were built from one platform to the next. These allowed priests or worshippers (or astronomers) to get from one level to the next.

It took sophisticated technology to build Mesopotamian ziggurats. Engineers had to calculate the area of each platform according to its length and width. They then had to calculate how many bricks were needed to build it: sun-dried bricks for the interior, and more durable kiln-fired bricks for the exterior. The brickwork was cemented together by clay or bitumen. Thick layers of reed matting stuffed among the layers of interior brickwork reinforced the structure.

THE ART OF TRANSPORTATION

Most people in ancient Mesopotamia lived near one of its two rivers, the Tigris or the Euphrates. These rivers flowed from north to south. Sailing boats could travel south on the rivers. The winds, and the flow of the rivers, were against them going north. To travel north, Mesopotamians had to go mainly by land. To make travel by land easier, in the fourth millennium BC, they made one of history's most important inventions: the wheel.

River Transport

The Tigris and the Euphrates were the highways of Mesopotamia. As the channels of the rivers changed (as a result of flooding, for example), people moved to stay near them. Life in ancient times in Mesopotamia depended on the rivers. Riverboats were the most common way to get around the area.

An Assyrian relief from the Palace of Sennacherib in Nineveh, which was carved around the seventh century BC, shows a military campaign and rowers in a reed boat. Mesopotamians built boats by bundling together water reeds that grew in the marshes along the Tigris and Euphrates rivers.

A model clay sailboat found in a grave in the Mesopotamian city of Eridu shows the basic design of early Mesopotamian boats. The grave was dug sometime before 4000 BC, so Mesopotamians were building and using boats more than 6,000 years ago. The model boat was wide, with a shallow bottom, like a barge. Boats in Mesopotamia needed to be built like that so they could get around the shallow rivers and canals. The model also had places to put up a mast and tie on the rigging, as well as a seat for the sailor. Boats also had oars for rowing along the rivers. Sometimes oxen, donkeys, or people alongside the riverbanks were used to pull boats upstream. The largest boats were barges and ferries made of wood that were 20 to 30 feet (6 to 9 m) long. Wood was scarce, so most boats were smaller and made from bundles of water reeds.

The reeds that the Mesopotamians used for their boats grew in the marshes around the mouth of the Tigris and Euphrates rivers, the Shatt al Arab. Water reeds are hollow and naturally buoyant. To make the boats waterproof, their outside was covered in a layer of bitumen. Up to the end of the twentieth century, the Marsh

A Marsh Arab is pictured here in 1974 tying together reeds to erect a home. People living near Nasiriya, near the ancient city of Ur in southern Iraq, used water reeds in many of the same ways that their ancient ancestors did, such as in building boats and constructing houses.

The Royal Standard of Ur, dating from around 2600 BC, was discovered during the early twentieth-century excavation of the royal graves of the Mesopotamian city of Ur, one of the world's most important archaeological discoveries. Made from shell, red limestone, and lapis lazuli, and believed to have been carried by a wooden pole that has decayed, the standard has two main panels, one called War and the other called Peace. The Peace panel shows animals such as fish and goats being brought to a banquet. The War panel, pictured here, depicts the Sumerian army and war chariots. The wheels of the chariots have axles and two half-moon shaped disks that have been attached together to form a single round wheel.

Arabs of the Shatt al Arab still built the same kind of reed boats that their ancient Mesopotamian ancestors built thousands of years earlier.

Mesopotamians also built a smaller kind of boat called a coracle. It was made of reeds, tied together into a round shape, and waterproofed with bitumen. Probably only one person could fit into it. The *kelek* was bigger than the coracle and was made from tree branches such as willow. Animal hides covered the outside to keep the boat waterproof. Sometimes inflated goat skins, sewn together like pillows, were attached for more buoyancy.

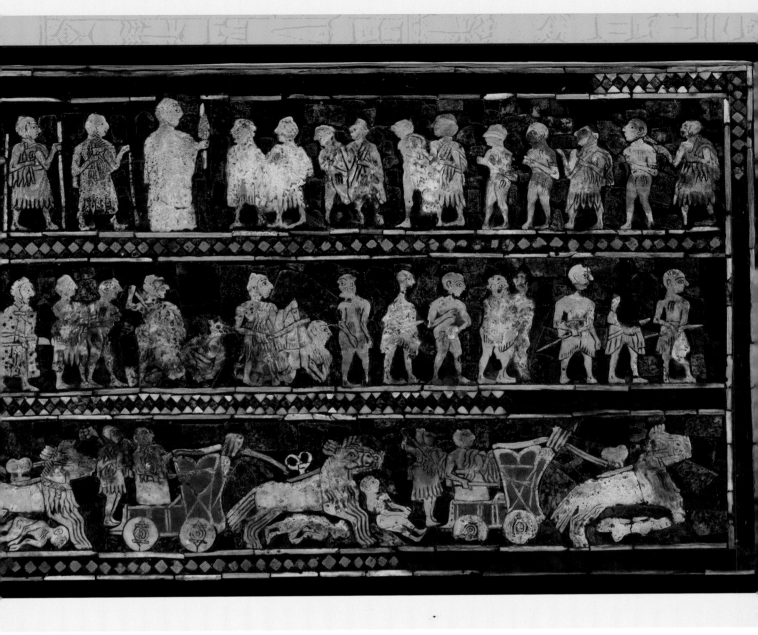

The Wheel

Mesopotamians invented the wheel in stages. Pictures on clay tablets from about 3200 BC show that, by then, Mesopotamians were using a kind of sledge with four basic wheels. From that time, the wheel evolved to become one of the most important inventions inherited from Mesopotamia. The vehicle wheel seems to have appeared in Mesopotamia around the same time as its cousin, the potter's wheel.

At first the Mesopotamians probably rolled heavy objects along on logs. This method required a lot of

An Assyrian war chariot from a relief in the Palace of Ashurbanipal (668–627 BC) in Nineveh illustrates the use of spoked wheels. Around 1500 BC the Mesopotamians found that they could bend strips of wood into round shapes by heating them. In this way they could make spoked wheels with wooden rims.

logs. It was a clumsy way to move things around. At some point, no one knows when, somebody probably thought it would be easier to cut away the middle part of the logs and leave just the round ends. A log axle, with its round "wheels" on each end, could be fitted to a cart. The wheels revolved with the axle. This wheels-and-axle device would make it much easier to pull a cart around.

By the third millennium BC, Sumerians were making wheels with two half-moon shaped disks of wood nailed together as a single round wheel. This was covered by some kind of animal hide (leather), like a thin tire, to protect the wood. The disk

AKKADIAN KING SARGON

According to legend, the first king of Akkad, Sargon (2340–2284 BC), wrote on a clay tablet that his mother placed him as a baby in a coraclelike basket to float him down the river:

> She set me in a wicker basket, with bitumen she made my opening watertight [waterproof].

> She cast me down into the river from which I could not ascend.

(From "Legends of the Kings of Akkade: The Texts,"
by J. G. Westenholz,
cited in Mesopotamia: The Invention of the City,
by Gwendolyn Leick).

was attached to the axle and revolved with it.

The most important stage in the evolution of the wheel came later in the third millennium or early second millennium BC, when the Mesopotamians put wheels on a fixed axle that revolved independently of it. The axle was now attached to the underside of the vehicle (a cart, for example), as it is on vehicles today. The wheels would be fitted onto the axle and could rotate freely around it. The wheels on one side of the vehicle could move at different speeds from those on the other side when the vehicle changed direction. This was a great advantage for vehicles needing to maneuver quickly (such as chariots in battle).

Solid wooden disk wheels evolved to spoked wheels around 1500 BC. The Mesopotamians discovered then that they could bend strips of wood into round shapes by heating them. So they began making wheels with round wooden rims. Spokes led out to the rim from the hub attached to the axle. This made wheels lighter (and probably stronger) so vehicles could be driven faster. These early spoked wheels were a little bigger than ordinary automobile wheels of today.

IRRIGATION AND AGRICULTURE

People settled around "the land between the rivers" for one reason: water. Water from the Tigris and Euphrates was necessary for life to survive in that otherwise dry desert region. It enabled people to grow crops and provided water for drinking.

The two rivers of Mesopotamia overflowed when rain in the north increased the flow of water running south to the sea. The overflowing rivers flooded the surrounding land. At those times of flood there was plenty of water to irrigate crops. The problem was that the rivers did not flood regularly. They could flood anytime between April and June. And a flood could be so overwhelming that it destroyed crops. Mesopotamians had to invent ways of getting water out of the rivers more regularly, and in controlled amounts, to irrigate their crops.

A picture from 1910 shows Egyptians working a shadoof. The Egyptians and Mesopotamians first used the shadoof around the same time, about 2000 BC. The long pole with a bucket on one end and a counterweight on the other was used mainly to irrigate fields.

They mastered the technology of irrigation. They built not only canals but underground aqueducts. They also built levees, or raised banks, along the rivers to protect against damaging floods. The basic materials used in water-supply projects were simple: baked brick and reeds. The design and organization of these projects, however, required sophisticated planning and engineering.

The Shadoof

The simplest form of irrigation was the shadoof (also spelled "shaduf"). It was invented in Mesopotamia and Egypt around 2000 BC, and is still used today in parts of the Middle East and Egypt. The shadoof consisted of a long pole with a bucket on one end and a counterweight on the other. The middle of the pole was set up on a wood framework. The farmer used his own weight to pull the bucket down into the river. When it filled up with water, the farmer let go of the bucket. The counterweight at the other end of the pole lifted the bucket up. The farmer could then swing the bucketful of water around and empty it into the canal used to irrigate his field. The system could also be used to transfer water from one big canal to another smaller one. A series of shadoofs could lift water in steps from a lower source of water to a higher level.

The Greek geographer Strabo (circa 64 BC–AD 23), in book 16 of his major work *Geography*, described a system used to irrigate the famous Hanging Gardens of Babylon (one of the Seven Wonders of the Ancient World). He described "water engines, by means of which persons, appointed for the purpose, are continually employed in raising water from the Euphrates into the garden." We cannot be certain what the "water engines" were. They may have been a series of shadoofs. Or they may have been part of a "bucket-and-chain" system. For this, a chain would be wound around two large wheels, one above the other. The wheels (and the chain) would revolve continuously. Buckets attached to the chain would lift water from the river in a continuous loop. They might have emptied directly into the gardens or into a channel leading into the gardens.

Canals

The Mesopotamians built extensive networks of canals. In the words of L. Sprague de Camp, in his book entitled *The Ancient Engineers* (1963), the Mesopotamian canal systems "tamed the mighty Euphrates, clothed the desert in rippling fields of golden grain, and moistened the roots of date palms planted along their banks." One of the most important responsibilities of rulers in Mesopotamia was to construct canals and levees to protect against flooding.

Canals were dug out by hand using primitive hand tools. The sides were lined with bricks. The slope of the canal had to be precise. If the slope was too steep, the water would flow too fast and erode the canal bed. The water level would then drop too low to flow out into the fields. If the slope was too gradual, water would flow too slowly and the canal

This stone relief depicts an aqueduct and channels or canals near Nineveh that are bringing water to a garden for irrigation. The scene is from the Palace of Ashurbanipal and dates from about 645 BC.

would clog up with silt. Surveyors had to calculate not only the slope of the canal but its depth and width, and the positioning of sluice gates along the sides to let the water out. A number of Babylonian clay tablets, most of which are housed at the British Museum in London, England, have been found showing calculations for digging a canal. These include the calculation of its slope based on its depth and width.

Aqueducts

In the eighth century BC, an Assyrian king, Sargon II (ruling 721–705 BC), discovered how to build underground aqueducts to transport water long distances. A surveyor first had to mark out a line on the ground in the direction

MESOPOTAMIAN "FARMER'S ALMANAC"

Around 1700 BC, a farmer's almanac of nearly 100 lines was written on a clay tablet. In it, a farmer gives his son instructions about how to grow good crops, including instructions about how to use the seeder plow and how to manage workers. Farmers in Mesopotamia knew about the benefits of crop rotation (periodically leaving fields fallow), to increase the soil's fertility. It seems, however, that they did not know the technique of fertilizing their fields to increase crop yields.

the water had to travel. At intervals along the line, vertical holes were dug into the ground at different depths. Teams of diggers then dug out horizontal channels underground between the holes. Many teams could dig out the underground channel faster than one digger burrowing along by himself like a mole. Workers then smoothed out the walls of the underground channel to turn the tunnel into an underground aqueduct.

This technology only worked in the hard rock of northern Mesopotamia. In the south the ground was muddy clay and could not be tunneled into without collapsing. Where they

needed to build aqueducts in the south, they built them aboveground.

The Plow

Cylinder seals were stone cylinders, about one or one and a half inches (three to four centimeters) long, engraved with the owner's design or imprint. The owner of the seal would mark his imprint into a clay object by rolling the seal over the clay when it was soft. The imprint left in the clay identified him as the owner.

Cylinder seals dating from the fourth millennium BC have been found with engravings of a plow. Plows might have been in use in Mesopotamia even

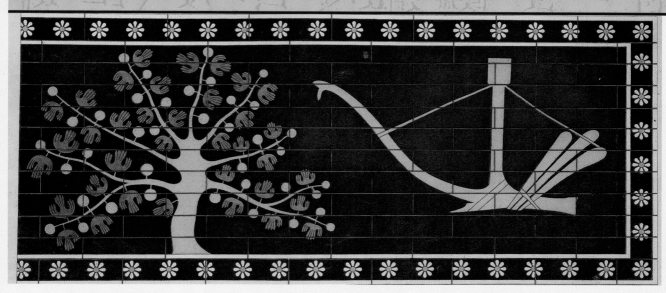

A Mesopotamian plow and fruit tree are seen in this nineteenth-century reconstruction of glazed tiles from the Palace of Nineveh. The earliest plow invented by the Mesopotamians was a simple device that just broke up the earth, allowing the farmer to drop seeds by hand into the ground. During the third millennium BC the Mesopotamians invented the seeder plow, which dropped seeds into furrows dug into the earth by the blade of the plow.

earlier, in the fifth millennium BC. The basic Mesopotamian plow was drawn by a pair of oxen and had a single pointed blade. It broke the surface of the ground, making a shallow furrow for seeds to be planted.

A more sophisticated version was the seeder plow, dating from the third millennium BC. This had a kind of funnel attached to it that allowed seeds to be dropped in place. As the farmer plowed, the seeds were covered with earth in their furrows. Three men were used to work the Mesopotamian seeder plow: one to steer the plow, another to guide the pair of oxen pulling it, and a third to drop the seeds into the funnel.

Barley was the most important grain crop in Mesopotamia. The Mesopotamians baked bread and made other foods from barley. They also used it to brew beer. Brewing technology was developed in Mesopotamia probably before 4000 BC.

THE TECHNOLOGY OF WRITING

The Mesopotamians invented writing 5,000 years ago. Scribes (writers) used a pointed stick or reed, called a stylus, to scratch pictures of things on damp clay tablets. This kind of writing was called cuneiform. The clay hardened, either baked by the sun or in a kiln. The writer's inscription lasted until the tablet crumbled or broke. For the duration of their civilization, throughout thousands of years, Mesopotamians wrote mainly on clay tablets. If scribes wanted to write something important, they used a stylus made from metal or bone to inscribe the writing on a more durable material such as stone. It was harder to do, but it lasted longer than clay tablets.

Hundreds of thousands of pieces of clay tablets with cuneiform writing have been found among the ruins of Mesopotamia. They show how cuneiform writing developed over thousands of years. At first the tablets recorded mostly activities revolving around

A scene from a stone relief from Nineveh, from about 700 BC, shows scribes with hinged writing boards and scrolls counting enemy heads after a battle. The Mesopotamians invented writing more than 5,000 years ago. They first used a stylus, which was a simple pointed water reed, to draw pictures of objects on wet clay tablets.

agriculture or the economy of early Mesopotamian cities. Some tablets contain lists of cuneiform words to teach others what the symbols meant. (At the time, there was no such thing as an alphabet. The world's first alphabet was invented in Palestine and Syria around 1700 BC.) Cuneiform was the standard form of writing throughout almost the entire period of Mesopotamian civilization.

From Pictograms to Cuneiform

The earliest Mesopotamian writing on clay tablets dates from about 3500 to 3000 BC. It features pictures of things like sheep or cattle or grain stored in a warehouse. Each picture symbol was a pictogram. A picture of an ox's head would be the pictogram for an ox. The pictogram for a day would be a picture of the sun coming over the

The three tablets pictured here represent the progression of the technology of writing in Mesopotamia. The top limestone tablet shows pictograms of proper names, including a landowner, and dates from the end of the fourth millennium. The middle clay tablet shows the grain counts at a temple. It dates from around 2900 BC, just before cuneiform writing was common, and uses pictures and symbols. The bottom clay tablet lists in cuneiform barley rations for seventeen gardeners for one month. The tablet dates from about 2000 BC.

horizon. Barley was represented as an ear of barley. The main reason writing was invented was to keep accounts and official records. It was only much later that writing was used for literary or artistic purposes.

Gradually, over hundreds of years, the Mesopotamians made their picture writing more abstract. They found it was easier to write a simplified symbol of an ox, for example, rather than a picture of it. They began using the end of a cut reed as a stylus to make standard marks to represent the object, rather than using a sharp point to draw a picture of it. The blunt end of a reed stylus was a wedge shape. The wedge-shape writing they produced was called cuneiform (from *cuneus*, the Latin word for "wedge").

A rounded cylinder seal and its imprint show imaginary animals and dates from the Uruk period of Mesopotamian history, around 3300 BC. Cylinder seals impressed an image onto wet clay and were used to identify an owner's possession, similar to an identification tag.

At first, cuneiform writing only represented objects or numbers. There was no grammar and no representation of the sounds of the spoken language. By around 2500 BC, cuneiform signs used for objects began to represent sounds, too. The sounds they stood for—syllables—were from the language of the dominant people of the time, the Sumerians. This was the beginning of writing that represented the spoken word. From then on, the different languages of people all around Mesopotamia began to be written in cuneiform script.

Clay Envelopes

The Mesopotamians not only invented writing, they invented stationery, too. From around 2000 BC, they started using clay envelopes in which to put the clay tablets they wrote on. The information inscribed on a clay tablet could easily be changed by wetting the clay and rewriting on it. Clay envelopes, sealed with an official clay seal, kept the documents safe. Personal "letters," written on a clay tablet and sealed, could also be put in clay envelopes. The address ("To my brother, Awil-Adad," for example) would be inscribed on the outside of the envelope. This would have been the world's first postal service!

Seals

Seals were used by the Mesopotamians even before writing. The earliest, from the sixth millennium BC, were in the form of flat stamps (stamp seals). The

CODE OF HAMMURABI

Some of the laws of the Code of Hammurabi are as follows:

Number 56: If a man lets in the water [from an irrigation canal], and the water overflows the field of his neighbor, he shall pay ten *gur* [330 gallons (1,249 liters)] for every ten *gan* [275 square yards (230 square m)] of land.

Number 121: If anyone stores grain in another man's house, he shall pay him five *silas* [7.5 pints (4.1 cubic decimeters)] for every *gur* [4.1 bushels (0.14 cubic meter)] of grain per year.

Number 195: If a son strikes his father, his [the son's] hands shall be cut off.

Number 196: If a man destroys the eye of another man, they will destroy his eye. (Or, as we commonly know it, "An eye for an eye . . .")

Number 198: If he puts out the eye of a freed man [a man of lower social status], or breaks the bone of a freed man, he shall pay one *mina* [18 ounces (510 grams)] of gold.

Number 200: If he knocks out the teeth of another man, his teeth shall be knocked out.

Number 248: If anyone hires an ox, and breaks one of its horns, or its tail, or hurts its muzzle, he shall pay one quarter of the value [of the ox] in money.

stamp had a design inscribed on it that identified its owner. Rounded cylinders (cylinder seals) came later, around the middle of the fourth millennium BC. Cylinder seals were made from a hard material such as bone or stone. The designs, such as a bundle of wheat or a head of an ox, were sometimes very elaborate.

The owner of the seal stamped or rolled it across a wet lump of clay that he or she used like a tag to identify, for example, a bag of the owner's grain or a jar of liquid. The design from the seal impressed into the clay tag identified the owner. By around 2400 BC, the seal was used to stamp the owner's sign, or name, on a clay tablet. It identified the person who had witnessed the transaction or information recorded on the tablet. Royal seals were stamped on writings to show that some document or activity was authorized by the king.

Hammurabi's Legal Code

Hammurabi (who ruled from 1792 to 1750 BC) was king of Babylon. He was one of the greatest of all Mesopotamian rulers. During his reign, 282 "laws" were engraved on a block of black granite stone that was 6.5 feet (2 m) tall. The laws, written in cuneiform in the Babylonian language, are known as the Code of Hammurabi. In fact, they were not laws as such. They were a series of people's rights, responsibilities and obligations, and legal judgments. Punishments for offenses were based on the concept of "an eye for an eye, a tooth for a tooth."

The Code of Hammurabi is the single most important written document of Mesopotamia. It gives us a clear view of everyday life and the organization of Babylonian society in the eighteenth century BC. It is the longest and most complete legal document in the history of Mesopotamia yet discovered. The stone on which the code was written was discovered by French archaeologist Jean-Vincent Scheil in 1901. Today it is housed in the Louvre Museum in Paris, France.

The Code of Hammurabi (1792–1750) is a collection of 282 case laws (violations of the law and their corresponding punishments), inscribed on a 6.5-foot-tall (2-m-tall) stela, discovered at Susa, in southern Iran, in 1901. At the top of the stela is a carving that shows Shamash (left), the sun god, handing the law to Hammurabi.

THE TECHNOLOGY OF MATHEMATICS AND NUMBERS

Our knowledge of the Mesopotamians' counting systems comes mainly from Babylonian times (2000–600 BC). Earlier, the Sumerians and Akkadians had used a counting system based on units of sixty (called a base-sixty, or sexagesimal system; today we mainly use a system based on units of ten, the decimal system). The Babylonians inherited the sexagesimal system and developed very complex mathematics from it. Today we still use the old Babylonian base-sixty system for some units of measurement; for example, there are sixty minutes in an hour and 360 degrees in a circle.

Before Babylon

Babylonian mathematics evolved over thousands of years from number systems in Mesopotamia. The earliest, from the seventh

MESOPOTAMIAN WEIGHTS AND MEASURES

Akkadian Name	Sumerian Name	English Translation	Equals
Weights			
1 she*	se*	grain	0.001/66 oz (0.05 g)
1 shiklu	gin	shekel	180 she = 0.3 oz (9.3g)
1 manu	ma-na	mina	60 shiklu = 18 oz (560 g)
1 biltu	gu	talent	60 manu = 67 pounds (30.4 kg)
			(* pronounced "shay")
Measures			
1 ubanu	shu-si	finger	0.6666 inch (1.7 cm)
1 ammatu	kush	cubit	24 ubanu = 15.5 inches (39.4 cm)
1 kanu	gi	reed/cane	6 ammatu = 7 feet 10.5 inches (2.4 m)
1 gar	gar-(du)	**	12 ammatu = 15 feet 9 inches (4.8 m)
1 ashlu	esh	line	10 gar = 52.5 yards (48 m)
1 beru	danna	league	1800 gar-(du) = 5.25 miles (8.5 km)
			(** no English equivalent)

(Adapted from *Handbook to Life in Ancient Mesopotamia* by Stephen Bertman)

millennium BC, involved the use of simple clay tokens. The number of tokens represented a number of sheep, or bundles of grain, or some other agricultural commodity. Tokens later came to represent a fixed number of something. A cone-shaped token might mean ten sheep. Two cone tokens would represent twenty sheep. A round token might represent fifty

This Sumerian clay tablet gives the calculations of the surface area of land at the city of Umma, and dates from 2100 BC. The Mesopotamians used cuneiform tablets to write down the conversion tables of complex mathematical problems, including trigonometry, by 1700 BC.

bundles of grain. Three round tokens meant 150 bundles of grain.

The invention of cuneiform writing around 3000 BC brought an important change in Mesopotamian counting. In the past, one symbol would represent a number and the thing being counted; for example, one symbol for five sheep, and a different symbol for five bundles of grain. Now the symbol for the quantity of something could be written in cuneiform. That would be followed by a separate symbol for the item being counted.

This was the beginning of numbers and measuring systems. Over the third millennium BC, the Mesopotamians developed many different systems of weights and measures. (Even today we use different measuring systems; for example, kilograms and pounds, meters and feet, and acres and hectares.) They used cuneiform tablets to record not only amounts but also mathematical calculations, such as the formula for the area of a field, or the length of a city wall. They also made up conversion tables with solutions to all kinds of complicated mathematical problems. By 1700 BC there were thousands of clay tablets showing multiplication tables, square roots, and other complex mathematics, including trigonometry.

Tables helped people count large or complex numbers in the sixty-base (sexagesimal) system. Although the system was written using just two cuneiform marks, the vertical wedge sign and the horizontal wedge sign, it could be used to calculate some very sophisticated mathematics, including square roots, algebra, and the value of pi (the ratio of the circumference of a circle to its diameter) to calculate the area of a circle.

We have inherited important features of Mesopotamian counting systems. The division of the hour into sixty minutes and the minute into sixty seconds, as well as the 360 degrees of a circle, come from the Mesopotamian sexagesimal system. The division of the day into twenty-four hours, and the year into 365 days, also comes from ancient Mesopotamia.

Conclusion

The Mesopotamian civilization ended when Islam emerged as the most powerful cultural force in the region around AD 650. The great cities and structures built by the Mesopotamians were abandoned. The magnificent palaces, gardens, canals, and ziggurats of Sumer, Akkad, and Babylon crumbled into ruins. They remained covered by the desert sands until their discovery by archaeologists in the nineteenth century. Technologies that evolved in Mesopotamia over many thousands of years, however, survived the passage of time. They were passed on and developed by later civilizations of ancient Greeks and Romans, Persians, North Africans, and modern Europeans. Today many of the most basic technologies that we take for granted—for example, the wheel, writing, and counting systems—were born thousands of years ago in "the land between the rivers," that cradle of civilization that we know as Mesopotamia.

TIMELINE

10,000–9000 BC	Permanent settlements begin in the region around Mesopotamia.
7000 BC	First farming communities are created.
7000–6000 BC	Earliest counting system (clay tokens) is used.
6000 BC	Handmade pottery and clay stamp seals are made.
3500–3200 BC	The wheel is invented for pottery making and transportation.
circa 3500 BC	First picture writing appears; cylinder seals are used.
3200–2000 BC	Early Bronze Age takes place in Mesopotamia.
circa 3200 BC	Earliest Mesopotamian city, Uruka, flourishes.
circa 3000 BC	Cuneiform writing is invented.
circa 2500 BC	Cuneiform symbols begin to represent sounds and speech.
2100 BC	Ziggurat of Ur is constructed.
circa 1755 BC	Code of King Hammurabi (1792–1750 BC) is engraved in cuneiform on a stone slab.
circa 604–562 BC	The reign of King Nebuchadrezzar II and the construction of the Hanging Gardens of Babylon occur.
539–331 BC	Babylon is ruled by Persians.
331–126 BC	Mesopotamia is ruled by the Greeks.
126 BC–AD 227	Parthians (early Iranians) rule Mesopotamia.
AD 75	Last known cuneiform text is written.
AD 227–651	Sassanian (later Iranian) period of rule occurs.
circa AD 651	Islamic conquest of Mesopotamia takes place; ancient Mesopotamian civilization ends.

GLOSSARY

archaeological Having to do with the remains and creations of ancient civilizations or cultures.

ascend Go up.

barrel vault Also called a tunnel vault, a ceiling or roof consisting of semi-cylindrical arches; it resembles a barrel or tunnel that has been cut in half lengthwise.

buoyant Able to float.

communal Shared by the whole community.

elaborate Complex, made with a lot of detail.

fallow Referring to land left uncultivated to reclaim its fertility.

gypsum A mineral that, when dried by intense heat, becomes plaster powder.

kiln An oven used for firing (baking) pottery, bricks, and other clay objects.

millennium A period of 1,000 years, especially between whole number periods, for example, 3000–2001 BC, 4000–3001 BC, AD 1001–2000, etc.

scarce Hard to find; in short supply.

sexagesimal A counting system based on units of sixty (compared with, for example, the decimal system based on units of ten).

slope The downward (or upward) angle of something, relative to the horizontal.

technology The technique, skill, or knowledge used to create something.

urban Having to do with cities.

ziggurat A temple tower built in stepped tiers to a high peak.

FOR MORE INFORMATION

The British Museum
Great Russell Street
London WC1B 3DG
England
44 (0)20 7323 8000
Web site: http://www.thebritish
museum.ac.uk

The Metropolitan Museum of Art
1000 Fifth Avenue
New York, NY 10028-0198
(212) 535-7710
Web site: http://www.metmuseum.org/
visitor/index.asp

The Oriental Institute
University of Chicago
1155 East Fifty-Eighth Street
Chicago, IL 60637
(773) 702-9514 (General Information)
(773) 702-9520 (Museum)

Web site: http://oi.uchicago.edu/OI/
default.html

The University of Pennsylvania
Museum of Archaeology and
Anthropology
3260 South Street
Philadelphia, PA 19104
(215) 898-4000
Web site: http://www.museum.upenn.
edu

Web Sites

Due to the changing nature of Internet
links, the Rosen Publishing Group, Inc.,
has developed an online list of Web
sites related to the subject of this book.
This site is updated regularly. Please use
this link to access the list:

http://www.rosenlinks.com/taw/teme

FOR FURTHER READING

Beek, M. A. *Atlas of Mesopotamia*. New York, NY: Thomas Nelson, 1962.

Bottero, J., et al. *Everyday Life in Ancient Mesopotamia*. Baltimore, MD: Johns Hopkins University Press, 2001.

Brown, Dale M. *Mesopotamia: The Mighty Kings*. New York, NY: Time-Life Books, 1995.

Burenhult, Goran, ed. *Great Civilizations*. San Francisco, CA: Fog City Press, 2004.

Frankfort, H. *The Birth of Civilization in the Near East*. New York, NY: Doubleday, 1956.

Glassner, J.-J. "Progress, Science and the Use of Knowledge in Ancient Mesopotamia." In *Civilizations of the Ancient Near East*, edited by Jack M. Sasson, et al. New York, NY: Scribner's, 1995.

Kramer, Samuel Noah. *Cradle of Civilization*. Alexandria, VA: Time-Life Books, 1967.

Kramer, Samuel Noah. *History Begins at Sumer: Twenty-Seven "Firsts" in Man's Recorded History*. Philadelphia, PA: University of Pennsylvania Press, 1981.

Meyers, E. M., ed. *The Oxford Encyclopedia of Archaeology in the Near East*. New York, NY: Oxford University Press, 1997.

Roaf, Michael. *Cultural Atlas of Mesopotamia and the Ancient Near East*. New York, NY: Facts on File, 1990.

BIBLIOGRAPHY

Bertman, Stephen. *Handbook to Life in Ancient Mesopotamia*. New York, NY: Facts on File, 2003.

Civil, Miguel. "Modern Brewers Recreate Ancient Beer," Autumn 1991. Retrieved November 24, 2004 (http://oi.uchicago.edu/OI/IS/CIVIL/NN_FAL91/NN_Fal91.html).

De Camp, L. Sprague. *The Ancient Engineers*. New York, NY: Ballantine, 1963.

Hart-Davis, Adam. "Mesopotamia." *What the Past Did for Us*. London, England: BBC Books, 2004.

Leick, Gwendolyn. *Mesopotamia: The Invention of the City*. London, England: Penguin Books, 2002.

Melville, Duncan J. "Mesopotamian Mathematics: Chronology of Mesopotamian Mathematics," May 2001. Retrieved December 1, 2004 (http://it.stlawu.edu/%7Edmelvill/mesomath/chronology.html).

O'Connor, J. J., and E. F. Robertson. "An Overview of Babylonian Mathematics." Retrieved November 2004 (http://www-groups.dcs.stand.ac.uk/~history/HistTompics/Babylonian_mathematics.html).

Reade, Julian. *Mesopotamia*. London, England: The British Museum Press, 2000.

Walker, C. B. F. *Reading the Past: Cuneiform*. London, England: The British Museum Press, 2004.

Wiltshire, Katharine. *Timeline of the Ancient World: Mesopotamia, Egypt, Greece, Rome*. London, England: The British Museum Press, 2004.

INDEX

About the Author

Graham Faiella has written many nonfiction books. He has a keen interest in the history, myths, cultures, and technology of the ancient world. Originally from Bermuda, Mr. Faiella has lived in London, England, since graduating with an MA degree in Italian and Hispanic Studies from Edinburgh University in Scotland in 1978.

Photo Credits

Cover © The British Library/Topham/The Image Works; cover (inset), pp. 9 (left), 24, 34 (top & bottom), 35, 40 Erich Lessing/Art Resource, NY; p. 4 Iraq Museum, Baghdad/Bridgeman Art Library; p. 7 Originally published in Historical Atlas of the World, © J. W. Cappelens Forlag A/S, Oslo, 1962. Maps by Berit Lie. Used with permission of J.W. Cappelens Forlag; pp. 9 (right), 22–23, 29 © The Trustees of The British Museum; p. 10 akg-images; pp. 13, 20 The Art Archive/Musée du Louvre Paris/Dagli Orti; p. 14 akg-images/Gérard Degeorge; p. 16 Scala/Art Resource, NY; p. 17 © Topham/The Image Works; p. 21 © Nik Wheeler/Corbis; p. 27 © Mary Evans Picture Library/The Image Works; p. 31 The Art Archive/Bibliothèque des Arts Décoratifs Paris/Dagli Orti; p. 33 © 2004 Werner Forman/TopFoto/The Image Works; p. 34 (middle) The Metropolitan Museum of Art, Purchase, Raymond and Beverly Sackler, 1988 (1988.433.1) Photograph © 2005 The Metropolitan Museum of Art; p. 36 Réunion des Musées Nationaux/Art Resource, NY.

Editor: Kathy Kuhtz Campbell
Designer: Evelyn Horovicz
Photo Researcher: Amy Feinberg